KU-012-491

First published 1986 by
Walker Books Ltd
184-192 Drummond Street
London NW1 3HP

Text © 1986 Judy Taylor
Illustrations © 1986 Peter Cross

First printed 1986
Reprinted 1986
Printed and bound by L.E.G.O., Vicenza, Italy

British Library Cataloguing in Publication Data
Cross, Peter
Dudley goes flying. – (Dudley the dormouse;2)
I. Title   II. Taylor, Judy   III. Series
823'.914[J]   PZ7

ISBN 0-7445-0458-9

DUDLEY
GOES FLYING

PETER CROSS

Text by
JUDY TAYLOR

WALKER BOOKS
LONDON

It was a cold night in Shadyhanger and there was the feeling of snow in the wind.

But Dudley was snug and warm. He had just woken up and was thinking about tea.

Dudley stoked up the fire and
put the kettle on to boil. Slowly
the room filled with smoke.

'I wonder if something is blocking the chimney?' thought Dudley. 'I'd better go up and see.'

Dudley took the lift to the top.
The tree was swaying in
the wind. *Going up...*

Second
branch...

first
branch...

As Dudley stepped out he was
buffeted by the wind and large
leaves swirled about his head.
It was a dangerous night
to be out.

The dark clouds cleared from the moon. Dudley saw at once what was wrong. The chimney was blocked with leaves.

Dudley wrapped his tail round the branch and swung down over the chimney. He might just be able to reach if he stretched out at full mouse length.

Dudley swung backwards and forwards, each swing bringing him nearer to the chimney. One last gust of wind and *bang!* he hit the top of the chimney very hard.

The leaves flew free and the smoke poured out but Dudley was falling quickly through the cold night air.

He grasped at a passing
leaf and slowed down with
an arm-pulling jerk.

Gently Dudley

and the

leaf

sailed

to the

ground.

Back inside his warm, snug house Dudley found the kettle boiling merrily. He made a large pot of tea – and ate a specially large piece of cake. Dudley began to think that it might soon be time for a nap.